Gorky Rises

WILLIAM STEIG

SQUARE
FISH

Farrar Straus Giroux
New York

To Delia, Sidonie, Nika,
Abigail, Sylvain, Estelle,
Kyle, Molly, and Reid

SQUARE
FISH

An Imprint of Macmillan

ISBN 978-0-374-42784-9
Library of Congress catalog card number: 80-68068

Originally published in the United States by Farrar Straus Giroux
First Square Fish Edition: August 2012
Square Fish logo designed by Filomena Tuosto
mackids.com

13 15 17 19 20 18 16 14

AR: 4.9 / LEXILE: AD690L

As soon as his parents kissed him goodbye and left, Gorky set up his laboratory by the kitchen sink and got to work. He took a clean tumbler, let in one squirt of water, and added first a little of this and then a little of that: a spoon each of chicken soup, tea, and vinegar, a sprinkle of coffee grounds, one shake of talcum powder, two shakes of paprika, a dash of cinnamon, a splash of witch hazel. He stirred vigorously and held the mixture up to the light. Too murky.

Very carefully, he put in a bit of his father's clear cognac. Better. But something still was missing. What?

Aha! Attar of roses. Gorky stepped out of his laboratory to fetch his mother's best perfume. He meant to use just a few drops; but, ravished by the scent of roses, he recklessly poured in all there was—half a bottle.

That did it! The thick stuff sank to the bottom of the mixing glass and he had a reddish-golden liquid full of tiny bubbles that glinted like particles of fire. *This,* obviously, was the magic formula he had long been seeking. With a steady hand, he decanted the pure bubbly part into the perfume bottle and firmly closed it with the glass stopper. Then he went out into the sunlight.

He set the bottle down on a tree stump not far from the house and arranged around it a circle of pebbles and fresh-picked daisies. Then he moved back a few paces and solemnly bowed to his magic liquid—once with his arms out sideways, once with his arms straight forward, once with his fingertips to his brow, and once touching his toes, each time saying, "Auga-looga, onga-ooga."

Sometime soon, he felt sure, he would learn exactly what sort of magic his bottle contained. He decided, meanwhile, to take it over to Elephant Rock, his best spot for doing nothing, and wait there for further developments.

He sauntered through a stretch of white clover, brushing the blossoms with his big feet. What a magical, cloverous smell! When he reached Poggle Brook, he stopped a moment to listen to the water. What magical music! He crossed the brook on the scattered stones and continued on his way.

It was early summer; everything was fresh and fair. The grass was green green; the sky was blue, immensely blue; the world was flooded with gracious light. No hurry about getting to Elephant Rock. Gorky spread himself out on the green green grass, facing the immensely blue sky, and just lay there, letting the sun include him in its warm embrace. The world was all magic, and he had a special bottle of it in his right hand.

A small, glittery snake came slithering through the grass, slid over Gorky's belly, circled his bottle three times, and wriggled off. Gorky grew hazy. He saw the clouds above as clean white clothes hung out to dry; and then he was asleep. The wide, open sky outside him was bright with brilliant sun, but the sky inside him shimmered with stars.

Whatever had kept him fastened to the earth let go its hold, and Gorky's slumbering body rose in the air, like a bubble rising in water, and moved off in an easterly direction.

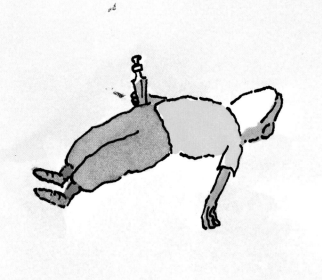

He woke up surrounded with sky, but he was unafraid. The green ground he had been resting on lay well below him, stretched out like an endless carpet; but feeling as airy as the air itself, he knew he would

not fall. It was clear now that he had indeed concocted a magic fluid. He could feel the brilliant bubbles flow into his arm from the bottle he held in his hand.

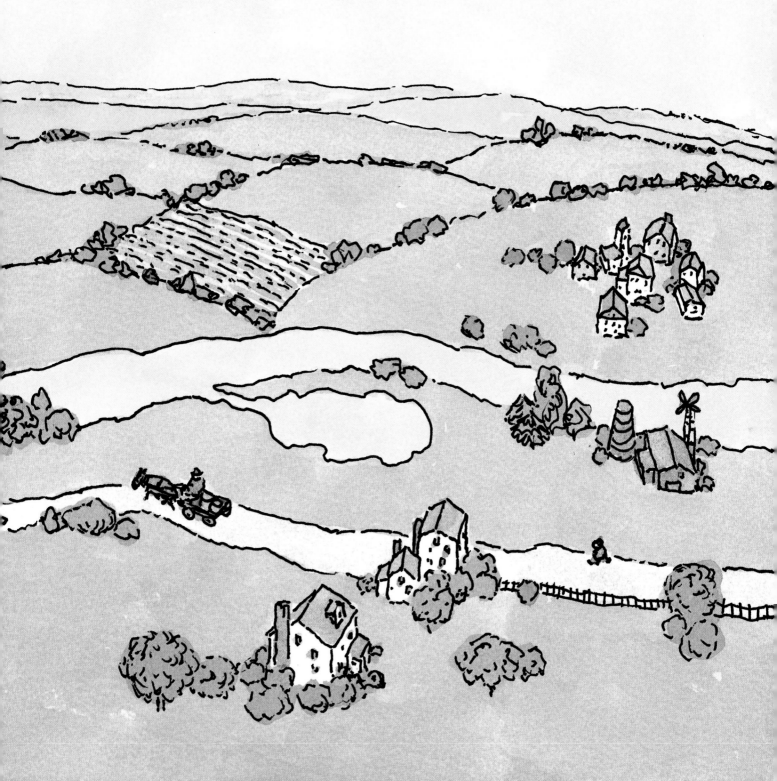

He was sailing through the air, very curious as to where he was heading, when a gruesome dragon and a monstrous butterfly came lunging and swiping at him. He almost croaked from fear, but these scary animals turned out to be kites!

Holding their strings down below were a couple of puppies. Gorky could see he had made quite an impression on them—they were prancing about like crazy, yapping and pointing his way. He waved to them once as he curved over some trees and out of their sight.

He was attracting more and more attention. Astonished, bewildered, and bedazzled eyes turned skyward as Gorky went soaring over the countryside, weaving through the air on a wavy course, sometimes higher, sometimes lower, sometimes this way, sometimes that. Farmers stopped their haying and stared up.

A pig in a rowboat dropped his fishing rod and stared up.

An artist stopped painting and stared up.

A bunny's swing halted in midair to give her time to stare up.

A fox dropped a goose he had just caught and stared up. The goose
ran off, but had to stop and stare up too.

As Gorky passed over Pruneville, they were craning their necks out of windows, running out of stores and houses, staring up from the streets. An old sea captain dug out his spyglass and fixed it on the mysterious creature sailing through the summer sky. (*What the doodad was keeping him up there?*) A house painter on a ladder, his brush dripping yellow, stopped his smearing to stare into the blue.

With the whole world watching, how could Gorky just do nothing? He stuck his thumbs in his armpits and crossed his eyes, he wiggled his hips, he clicked his heels together and twiddled his toes. Two rabbit aeronauts, swinging along in their balloon, were electrified from ears to scuts at the sight of a young frog floating by, upside down.

Leaving the rabbits flabbergasted, Gorky went swooping on a graceful downswing right over his cousin Gogol's lawn. And now he really felt like showing off! Gogol was out on the grass with his toys when Gorky came rolling by, turning in the air like a wheel on its axle. Gogol was goggle-eyed. He tore after his cousin, yelling, "Gorky! Gorky! What's up?"

"*I* am!" Gorky yelled back. And that's all he had time to say before he was whisked up into the sky again. Zooming along in the upper reaches of the atmosphere, he remembered Gogol's look of stupid wonder and couldn't stop laughing.

It was some time before he sobered up and noticed he was under a canopy of swarthy clouds that spread their gloom on the earth below. The peaceful blue sky had been left far behind.

Now, in sudden rage, a storm went wild around him. Lightning shattered the sky, thunder banged and bellowed, hailstones battered his body. He was tossed about by gusts of wind so strong they almost ripped his pants off. It was no frolic, and it went on and on until the hail gave way to great slapping raindrops as large as acorns.

What a relief when he finally found himself in blue sky again! He had been lifted high above the storm; faint lightning was visible in the clouds below and he could hear dim thunder. The storm was roving on, but he was barely drifting now.

Day faded. Half the sky flushed crimson. Then night spread far and wide. The lights of a town came on way beneath him and Gorky realized he was no longer moving at all, but was suspended in the heavens like a coat on a hanger.

He hung there a long, long time, wondering where he was—exactly what spot on the map he was over. There was nothing around him but the secret, silent night, the sea of blinking stars. Dreamily, he began asking himself questions he could not answer: Did anyone know where he was? Did God, for example, know? Did his parents? He wished he were home with them now, asleep in his feather bed. He was tired.

How could he get back down there, where he belonged? Could he *ever*

get back? It was the magic liquid that was keeping him aloft. What if he let it go? He would plummet straight to the ground, wouldn't he? He held the bottle tighter. He had to stay awake or he'd die with a shocking crash.

Morning was on its way, the sky beginning to lighten, when Gorky had an idea that shook him wide awake. What if he dripped out the liquid one drop at a time? Would the magic lose its grip little by little? He decided to find out.

He removed the stopper from the bottle and released one single drop. And he fell—ZAZOOM—then suddenly stopped!

Again, and the same thing happened—another drop from the bottle, another drop toward earth. On the third try he let out a few drops and took such a steep plunge he thought it was goodbye Gorky. It was just one at a time after that.

As the sun was coming up, Gorky, gratefully, was going down—drip and a drop, drip and a drop. Soon he was quite close to the dear solid ground. How good it looked! Was it part of the magic that he was directly over Elephant Rock? It had to be.

Two more drops and (one day late) he was sitting firmly on the rock itself. He'd had just enough liquid to reach the earth. No, there was one drop more. As he tilted the bottle, it made its appearance, waited on the lip a moment, and let itself fall on Elephant Rock.

And a most remarkable thing happened—in fact, a miracle! Elephant Rock began to quiver, and bestir itself. A large, fanlike ear spread out on each side, a trunk curled upward and trumpeted, and Gorky was astride a warm, live elephant that proceeded to walk away from the spot where it had been resting for the last ten million years.

It set out for Gorky's house, shuffling through the dewy grass.

Imagine the effect on Cousin Gogol when Gorky turned up again, this time on an elephant, after flying past without wings the day before.

Gorky's parents had been out all night searching for him. By now, they were so worried they were ready to kill themselves just to end their misery. They were scouring the terrain in the neighborhood of home, peering behind every bush, stone, and tree, and into every hole and crevice, no matter how tiny.

When they saw a tremendous elephant lumbering toward them with their son on its back, and were sure of what they were seeing, they tore over, crying, "Gorky darling! Dear Gorky! Where on earth have you been?"

"I haven't *been* on earth," said Gorky.

"You haven't been *where!*" his mother exclaimed.

"Who is this elephant?" his father inquired.

Gorky took a deep breath and went into his story.

His father wasn't buying any of it, and even his doting mother didn't seem to believe him. "Well," said Gorky, "this real-live elephant used to be Elephant Rock. There's no rock over there anymore."

"Bogwash," his father snorted. "No more Elephant Rock? This I've got to see."

When they got to the place where the rock used to be, Gorky's parents stood and stared some long seconds, first at the naked ground, then at the elephant. Their big mouths hung open, but no words came out.

At last Gorky's father said: "Well, son, you must be tired after all that flying. Let's go home and get some sleep."